For precious Jean – welcome! ~ DB

For Amaya ~ HJT

A Lothian Children's Book

Published in Australia and New Zealand in 2023
by Hachette Australia
Gadigal Country, Level 17, 207 Kent Street, Sydney NSW 2000
www.hachettechildrens.com.au

Hachette Australia acknowledges and pays our respects to the past, present and future Traditional Owners and Custodians of Country throughout Australia and recognises the continuation of cultural, spiritual and educational practices of Aboriginal and Torres Strait Islander peoples. Our head office is located on the lands of the Gadigal people of the Eora Nation.

ISBN: 978 0 7344 2208 8 (hardback)

Designed by Kirby Armstrong
Colour reproduction by Splitting Image
Printed in China by Toppan Leefung Printing Limited

WHAT TO DO

when you're not sure what to do

DAVINA BELL
+ HILARY JEAN TAPPER

LOTHIAN Children's Books

Gentle hands!

A bigger step.

A softer voice.

A big breath.

Hello!

A smile can make somebody's day.

Even if you really want to...

it might not be the best idea.

It's always good to ask first.

If you go out and about,
let someone know.

Remember to look up!

And look down.

Some things need careful hands.

Some things need
to be left alone.

Starting can be the hardest part.

It always feels good to finish.

Count to ten... and ten again.

Find a you-shaped space.

Let yourself!

Stay in one spot.

Someone will come.

Think about how you might feel.

It might not be how
you imagined...

At first.

Some things are over too quickly.

Some things take time.

But nothing lasts forever.

(Except love.)

Sometimes the best thing
to do is very small.

And sometimes...

It's nothing at all.